AR Quiz#: 47822
BL: 4.1
AR Pts: 1.0

ALL-AMERICAN PUPPIES

2

ON THE SCENT OF TROUBLE

Susan Saunders

Illustrated by Henry Cole

AVON BOOKS

An Imprint of HarperCollinsPublishers

Library of Congress Catalog Card Number: 00-103021
ISBN 0-06-440885-X

First Avon edition, 2001

❖

AVON TRADEMARK REG. U.S. PAT. OFF. AND IN OTHER COUNTRIES,
MARCA REGISTRADA, HECHO EN U.S.A.

Visit us on the World Wide Web!
www.harperchildrens.com

ON THE SCENT OF TROUBLE

CHAPTER ONE

Rosie yawned, curling up her bright pink tongue. Then she rolled over on her pillow, which was tucked cozily under the kitchen table.

"Ready for breakfast, Rosie?" asked John, her new human.

He was standing beside the stove, flipping pancakes. John was a big man with a reddish brown beard that put Rosie in mind of a chow she once knew, back in the city. But

John was a lot more easygoing than the chow had been.

Rosie's life was a lot easier altogether.

Just a few weeks earlier, the bristly gray puppy with one green eye and one blue had been stuffed into a cardboard box.

She'd been driven miles away from the city and the only home she'd ever known.

Then she'd been tossed out a car window, onto a strange street in a strange town called Buxton.

Which could have been the end of Rosie.

Luckily she was rescued by four other puppies, and they'd quickly become best friends.

Now she had her own house—not a big house, but big enough for her and John. She had her own backyard. There was always plenty to eat, and not all of it was dog food, either. John ran the best deli in Buxton. He saved his leftovers for Rosie and her friends Jake, Sheena, Fritz, and Tracker.

Jake was a mostly black Lab puppy with four white feet and a white-tipped tail. He lived three blocks away with Mr. Casey and Waldo, a grumbling old sheepdog.

Sheena's house was right behind Jake's. She was a dachshund puppy who barked a lot and was very proud of her silky brown hair.

Fritz was Sheena's next-door neighbor—a German shepherd, he was at least twice the size of the other puppies in the group. He was also the youngest, and sometimes he acted like a big baby.

Tracker was a beagle puppy with very long ears and the keenest nose in Buxton. He lived just off Main Street, not far from the bakery that his humans owned.

Every morning, all five puppies waited until their humans left for work. They met in the alley beside Fritz's house and explored the town from one end to the other.

Rosie had overslept that day. She scrambled out from under the table to gobble down the delicious pieces of pancake sprinkled with puppy kibble that John spooned into her bowl. Then she trotted to the back door. "Wo-o-oof?"

John was about to unlatch the square dog door for her when the wall phone rang.

Rosie fidgeted while John talked. "Hello . . . Hey, Greg."

Rosie knew that Greg was one of Fritz's humans.

"What's up?" John went on. "Good—my niece Vanessa's coming for a week."

Niece. There was that word again—John had been saying it a lot.

"Fritz and Rosie get along just fine," John said into the phone. "Of course he can stay here until you're back." He added, "I'm sure the only thing Vanessa would like better than one puppy is two puppies."

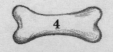

So maybe a niece was just another kind of puppy?

"She's nine years old," John was saying.

No, nine was definitely a full-grown dog, so Rosie's house was going to be crowded for a while.

But she wasn't worried. She could keep Fritz in line. And if the niece stayed out of Rosie's way, Rosie wouldn't bother her, either.

John hung up the phone, and pushed open the dog door.

"Good girl," he said as Rosie slid through it.

Wagging her tail, the gray puppy crossed the backyard to sit down under the pine tree.

She waited until John was backing his truck out of the driveway, on his way to work. Then she jumped up onto the stone barbecue pit. From there she leaped to the top rail of the picket fence. Rosie teetered along until she ran out of fence. She

hopped onto a big metal garbage can on the far side of it, and down to the sidewalk.

She made a quick stop at Mrs. Foster's, two houses over, for a snack. One sharp bark at the front door was enough—Mrs. Foster appeared with a chunk of blueberry muffin for Rosie.

"You are the sweetest little thing!" she exclaimed as the gray puppy chewed. "You are welcome at my house any time."

But Rosie was perfectly happy at John's.

She headed to the corner, still licking her lips. She turned onto the street where Fritz and Sheena lived.

Both puppies were already waiting for Rosie in the alley.

Sheena barked a shrill "hey-ey-ey."

Fritz was huddled against his fence, trembling.

"What's the matter with him?" Rosie asked the dachshund puppy.

"He's worried about being at your house," Sheena said.

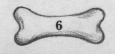

6

"It's a fine house!" Rosie rumbled at Fritz. "And nobody's a nicer human than John."

Sheena shook herself, and let her long hair fall neatly into place again before she spoke for the shepherd. "Fritz is scared of children."

"Children?" Rosie said, puzzled. "There aren't any children at our house. Just John and me."

"What about the niece?" Fritz groaned. One of his ears was standing straight up, but the other drooped weakly.

"A niece is a *kid*?" Rosie said.

She hadn't been around kids much herself, but she'd met a few in the city. Sometimes they were noisy and grabby, especially the smaller ones. But sometimes they shared snacks with puppies, or threw a ball. And they never got tired.

Just then Jake and Tracker galloped into the alley.

"What's going on?" the Lab puppy asked,

glancing at the shivering shepherd.

"Have those cats been hassling you, Fritz?" said the beagle puppy.

Puffy and Mr. Purr, the bakery cats, loved to spring out at Fritz and scare him silly.

Sheena said, "It's not the cats. Fritz is going to stay at Rosie's for a few days, and . . ."

". . . and a kid will be there, too." Rosie finished for her.

"Is that all?" said Jake. "Mr. Casey has two grandkids, and they're not so bad." After a moment he added, "At least, the bigger one's okay. The little one pulls my tail."

Fritz was whining now.

"Rosie will take care of you," Jake told the shepherd.

"I can handle just about anything—I'm a city dog," Rosie reminded him. "Plus there'll be two of us. Two pups and only one kid means no problem."

The shepherd puppy sat up a little straighter. "Two against one," he repeated.

"That's right," said Rosie.

Fritz wagged his tail a couple of times.

"Okay, that's settled. So where are we going this morning?" said Jake.

"To the river, to growl at water rats?" said Sheena.

"Or the dump, to bark at woodchucks?" said Tracker.

"Woodchucks!" the five puppies agreed.

They set off for the dump on the far side of town.

CHAPTER TWO

Rosie was pretty tired after chasing woodchucks around the dump for a couple of hours. When John showed up at the house on his lunch break, she was under the table on her pillow, snoring away.

"Are you getting enough exercise?" John wondered aloud. "Wake up, Rosie—I brought you a little something to eat."

As they shared a few slices of deli roast beef, a car pulled up at the curb in front.

Greg and Marcia climbed out of it and started up the walk.

Marcia was carrying Fritz. Greg was carrying Fritz's beanbag bed, his food and

water bowls, a huge container of special kibble, and a brand-new stuffed teddy bear.

John opened the front door for them.

Fritz was whimpering, and so was Marcia.

"Please don't cry, Fritzie," she murmured in the shepherd's droopy ear. "We'll call every night to see how you're doing. Oh, Greg—maybe I should stay at home with him."

"Marcia, it's *your* sister who broke her ankle line dancing," Greg pointed out.

He took Fritz from her and set the puppy down in the front hall. "Be brave, boy. You've got Rosie for company, and we'll be back before you know it."

"Vanessa will keep both of them busy," John said.

Which made Fritz whine even louder, especially after Greg and Marcia stepped outside again. The shepherd puppy tried to squeeze through the screen door after them, but John closed it, fast.

"Go on," John told them. "Don't worry

about Fritz. He'll settle down as soon as you're out of sight."

After John said good-bye to Greg and Marcia, he spread Fritz's beanbag bed near Rosie's pillow, at the end of the kitchen table. He lined up Fritz's dishes next to hers in front of the washing machine. Then he handed each of the puppies a Cheddar

cheese cracker from the deli.

"I have to get back to work," John said. "But I'll be home early."

Fritz wolfed down the biscuit and sobbed himself to sleep on his bed.

Rosie curled up on her pillow.

If Fritz was already so upset, how would he act when the kid came?

Rosie's eyes slowly closed. . . .

A sharp, high voice exclaimed, "*I* want to carry my backpack, Uncle John!"

Rosie woke with a start.

"Whe-ere am I?" Fritz mumbled sleepily beside her.

"At my house, and look out!" Rosie warned the shepherd puppy. "I think the kid's here already!"

There was a clatter of footsteps in the front hall.

"Which way's my room?" said the high voice.

"I'll show you. But come into the kitchen

first and meet Rosie," John said. "And Fritz."

"No-o-o!" Fritz groaned. He scrambled under the table, trying to squeeze between Rosie and the wall.

Normally Rosie would have run to meet John. But she stayed with Fritz, even when John called her.

"Rosie girl?" John said, walking into the kitchen. "This is Vanessa."

A round head covered with curly reddish hair appeared under the table.

"Rosie? Is she nice?" the kid said in her high voice—she had a couple of teeth missing.

"The best," said her uncle. "Why don't you pat . . ."

But Vanessa was backing away. The kid was actually afraid of them!

"The brown one's so big!" Vanessa said. "And why's he making that noise? Is he growling?"

Fritz was moaning softly.

"No, he's crying—he's kind of timid," John told her. "Rosie, come say hello."

Rosie eased out from under the table, both eyes on Vanessa.

"Funny eyes," Vanessa said nervously.

"Let her smell your hand," John directed.

Carefully, Vanessa stretched out her hand.

Just as carefully, Rosie sniffed at her fingers. Not too bad—Vanessa smelled like hard candy and bubble gum. Maybe she'd be a good source of treats.

There was another scent, too, something that Rosie hadn't smelled before. . . . The puppy edged closer to the backpack that was leaning against Vanessa's leg.

"Bad dog!" Vanessa said, snatching up the backpack and holding it high in the air.

"She's just trying to get to know you, Van," John said.

"Well, I don't want her sticking her nose in my backpack," Vanessa said.

Rosie didn't care for her tone—the puppy's top lip curled up.

"Uh-uh, Rosie," John murmured, and to Vanessa, "I had no clue that you'd never been around dogs before."

"Mom and Dad don't like any kind of pets," Vanessa said.

"Well, I have a feeling you and Rosie will be great friends," John said. "Come on—

you'll be sleeping upstairs, in my room. I'll stay in the spare room while you're here."

John headed out of the kitchen. He carried Vanessa's big suitcase, but she hung onto her backpack like it was crammed with fresh chew toys that she didn't want to share.

"Those dogs can't get into my room, can they?" she asked as they started up the stairs.

"The puppies aren't allowed off the first floor," John told her.

"Is there a door I can close?" Vanessa wanted to know.

"Absolutely," John said.

"Is sh-she g-gone?" Fritz stammered at last. He was still crouched under the table.

"She's a lot more worried about us than you need to be about her," Rosie growled at him. "Pull yourself together, Fritz! Act your size!"

CHAPTER THREE

Rosie and Fritz didn't see much of Vanessa that evening.

John took his niece to dinner and then to a movie on Main Street.

With Vanessa out of the house, Fritz relaxed a little. Rosie showed him around downstairs. She even encouraged him to jump onto the living-room couch and bark at the squirrels outside the window.

And then Marcia called.

The puppies listened to her voice on the answering machine: "Fritzie, are you there? How are you doing?"

"Awful! Ple-e-ease come and get me!"

moaned the shepherd puppy.

"We miss you, and we wish you were here," Marcia went on, sounding quavery.

"Just a few more days, pal," Greg added in the background.

Fritz crawled back under the table, whimpering. He was still at it when John and Vanessa got back.

"Maybe you'd like to spend some time with the puppies now," John suggested to his niece. "You could throw Rosie's ball for them."

Rosie grinned and wagged her tail—she loved chasing a ball.

But the girl shook her head and gave a loud yawn. "I'm really tired, Uncle John," she said.

"You have had a long day, sweetie," said her uncle, hugging her. "There's time for playing tomorrow."

But if Vanessa was so tired, why didn't she sleep?

The big bedroom was right above the

kitchen, where the puppies slept. It sounded as if the kid was moving furniture all night long. Moving furniture and giggling.

"What could she be doing?" Fritz whined, staring up at the ceiling fearfully.

"How would I know? Has to be a kid thing," Rosie said crossly.

The gray puppy finally dozed off.

But Vanessa woke Rosie up again. She came downstairs in the middle of the night to dig through the refrigerator for a slice of deli roast beef.

At breakfast time the kid looked pretty sleepy.

Rosie was dog tired herself. While Vanessa and John sat at the table and ate their cereal and bananas, Rosie crunched drowsily on kibble.

Fritz didn't touch his food. The shepherd stayed half-hidden between the clothes dryer and the trash can, as far away from Vanessa as possible.

As the humans got ready to leave for the

deli, Vanessa said, "You're sure the puppies can't push my door open, Uncle John?"

"You don't have to worry," John answered. "Rosie has never even been up the stairs, Van."

Rosie had never had any reason to go up there. Her pillow and her food and toys were all on the first floor. Plus the stairs were steep, and hard for a puppy to climb.

But now she was beginning to wonder. . . . Was there something in the kid's room that she didn't want the puppies to find?

Rosie waited until she heard John's truck rattling up the street, with John and Vanessa safely on board.

Then she said to Fritz, "Let's check it out!"

The shepherd puppy was finally eating his kibble. "Check . . . what . . . out?" he said around a mouthful.

"The kid's room," said Rosie.

"No way!" Fritz yelped. "You heard John—he doesn't want us upstairs!" He

licked the last crumb from his bowl and hurried over to the dog door. "Anyway, it's time to meet the guys."

Fritz squeezed through the opening before Rosie could argue with him.

Jake, Tracker, and Sheena watched Rosie and Fritz plod up the alley toward them.

"You look awful!" Sheena said. "Your hair is rumpled . . ."

". . . your eyes are dull, your noses dry . . ." said Tracker.

". . . like you haven't slept in days," Jake added.

"The kid's at John's already," Rosie told them.

"And kids can definitely wear you out," Sheena said wisely.

"So what are we doing this morning?" Jake asked.

"Let's go to the lake," said Tracker. "We can wade in the water, stir up the frogs . . ."

". . . take a nap in the shade?" said Rosie, too tired to imagine anything livelier.

But once she was squishing around in the oozy lake mud, the gray puppy perked up. Poking her nose into the weeds to make the bullfrogs jump, chasing big purple dragonflies, Rosie forgot all about Vanessa for a while.

The time passed so quickly that Rosie and Fritz barely made it into the yard before John's truck rolled up the driveway again.

John and Vanessa climbed out.

"I hope you puppies have been soaking up some sun," John said. He opened the back door for them all. "Let's get our hands washed for lunch, Vanessa."

He ruffled Rosie's fur on his way to the stairs. He was whistling a happy tune.

But a few seconds later John was bellowing, "Vanessa! What's happened to your room?"

He'd never sounded like that before. Rosie wondered what the kid could have done.

Vanessa slammed the refrigerator door. When she ran toward the stairs herself, Rosie noticed a chicken wing sticking out of her pocket.

The gray puppy dashed into the hall to hear the humans better.

"What a huge mess!" John was saying on the second floor.

"I guess I . . ." Vanessa began.

"I know *you* didn't do it," John

interrupted her. "I looked in before we left for the deli this morning, and the room was as neat as a pin! And I didn't do it, so . . . It couldn't have been Rosie—she's been living here for weeks already, and she always behaves herself when I'm out of the house. So it must have been Fritz, upset about Greg and Marcia leaving him behind!"

There was a long, low moan from the shepherd puppy, still lurking in the kitchen.

"Fritz?" Vanessa said. "Oh. The big puppy. I guess he . . . uh . . . must have pushed the door open and . . ."

John was already storming down the stairs.

Rosie raced back into the kitchen and jumped onto her pillow.

Fritz had crawled halfway under his beanbag bed with his teddy bear. He lay there, quivering, while John talked to him sternly.

"I know you're sad, Fritz. But I can't have my house torn apart," John said.

He lifted the beanbag bed off the shepherd puppy's head. "You knocked all of the books off the shelves. You ripped a big hole in the chair. You tipped over the ivy plant and scattered dirt everywhere! I'm really surprised at you." John went on, "If this happens again, I'll have to think about . . . about taking you to a kennel."

Fritz cried as if his heart were breaking.

"If Greg and Marcia call tonight, maybe I'll talk to them about enrolling you in obedience class," John added.

Rosie had heard about obedience classes from Sheena: getting bossed around by strangers, having to do silly stuff dogs would never do on their own.

Poor Fritz didn't deserve it. Who did?

Vanessa edged into the kitchen and stood near the refrigerator. She peered under the table at Fritz with a strange expression on her face.

Was she just feeling sorry for him? Or did she know he was being blamed unfairly?

A growl was forming deep in Rosie's throat. . . .

John heard her. "No, Rosie!" he said sharply. "Are Fritz's bad habits rubbing off on you? Maybe it would be a good idea to sign both of you puppies up for obedience classes!"

Vanessa shrugged at Rosie.

Then she quietly opened the refrigerator door, lifted out a hard-boiled egg, and headed up the stairs.

CHAPTER FOUR

"Start again, at the beginning," Jake said the next morning. He and Tracker and Sheena were standing in the alley outside Fritz's empty house, and they were all ears.

"Don't leave anything out," Tracker added.

They listened carefully as Rosie went over everything that had happened since Vanessa arrived two days earlier—Fritz was still too upset to make sense.

"I sniffed her hand when she walked into the kitchen that first day," Rosie said, "and she smelled like . . ."

". . . candy and bubble gum," said Sheena.

28

"Right," said Rosie.

"Any other scents?" the beagle puppy asked.

"Hmmm . . ." Rosie suddenly remembered the other smell that had been clinging to the kid's fingers. "Yeah, something different, musty-dusty. And it smelled stronger near her backpack," the gray puppy said.

"Kid smell?" Jake said to Tracker.

"She snatched her backpack away from me and carried it upstairs before I got a really good whiff," said Rosie.

"Kids can be tricky," Tracker said.

Sheena said, "So maybe she didn't want you and Fritz to go into her room because . . ."

". . . because we might find whatever it was she'd hidden in her backpack?" Rosie said.

"You're sure it wasn't food?" said Jake. He was always hungry. "Maybe some sharp cheese?"

"No way," Rosie said.

"Interesting," said Tracker.

Rosie said, "That night, which was the night before last—"

"There was giggling and furniture moving, right?" Sheena interrupted.

"Uh-huh," Rosie said. "Yesterday morning we went to the lake with you guys, and when we got back . . ."

"Disaster," said Sheena, scratching her ear with a hind foot. She smoothed her hair back down with her toenails.

"But I didn't do anything," Fritz murmured sadly. He'd been saying that over and over again.

"What I can't figure out is, how did the room get wrecked without anyone being at home?" Jake said.

The five puppies looked at each other. No one had a real answer.

"Tricks," Fritz said. "Scary kid tricks." He shivered.

"Kids aren't magic," Rosie muttered. *Are they?*

"What about last night?" Jake said.

"Nothing happened at all," said Rosie. "No noises, and no mess when the humans woke up this morning. But I have a bad feeling . . . which is why Fritz and I are going back right away, to keep an eye on the house."

"I'll go with you," Jake told his friend Rosie.

"I will, too—maybe I can track down that smell," the beagle puppy said.

"Count me in," Sheena said.

The five puppies got back into the yard the same way that Rosie and Fritz had been getting out: One by one they jumped up on top of the metal garbage can near the sidewalk, then onto the picket fence rail. They teetered along until they could leap over to John's stone barbecue pit and down to the grass.

"Let me go in first," Tracker said once they were gathered outside Rosie's back door. "Smell the smells while they're fresh."

The others waited while the beagle puppy slid through the dog door into the house. Suddenly he yelped loudly in surprise.

"Tracker, what is it?" Rosie barked. Then she sprang through the dog door herself, and lost her breath completely: The kitchen looked as though it had been hit by a whirlwind!

"Who? Wh-wha . . ." Rosie stammered. She couldn't begin to make sense of it.

The trash can was lying on the floor with the lid off. Garbage was strewn from one end of the room to the other.

Almost every cabinet had been opened: Flour, sugar, coffee, and rice had been spilled all over the counters. Bottles of pickles and mustard and vinegar lay broken on the floor.

Tracker wrinkled his nose. "It's hard to smell anything but this spicy stuff."

Jake was the next puppy inside. "Wow! Rosie!"

Then Sheena joined them. "This is really bad!"

Fritz tumbled through the door, too, and howled at the top of his lungs, "John'll take me straight to the kennel! No—to the animal shelter! He'll give me away!"

And suddenly Tracker yodeled, "I see it! Over the stove . . ."

"Where?" Then Rosie spotted the strange creature herself.

From the cabinet above the stove, the puppies were being watched closely by a

slender, silvery animal. It had a sharp nose, tiny ears, and a strip of dark fur across its bright black eyes, like a mask.

It wasn't a rat—it had a long, puffy tail.

And it wasn't a squirrel—its tail wasn't *that* puffy, plus its teeth were small and pointy instead of big and square.

Rosie didn't know what the animal was. Or how it had gotten into her kitchen!

All at once she was boiling mad. She growled louder than she'd ever growled in her life.

The creature stood up on its hind legs and glared straight at her.

That's when Rosie spotted the narrow blue collar around its neck.

A collar meant "pet." But *whose?* And a pet *what?*

The animal flicked its tail and hissed, like a cat!

"Bow-wow-wooow!" Rosie barked.

Sheena and Jake and Tracker took up the cry.

Fritz scuttled under the table.

Rosie threw herself furiously at the stove, trying to get close enough to grab the animal with her teeth. But it scurried along the top shelf, out of reach, tossing cans and bottles out of the cabinet as it went.

The puppies were making so much noise that they didn't hear the footsteps in the hall.

Suddenly the kitchen door swung wide open, and John and Vanessa were standing there.

"HAVE . . . ALL . . . OF . . . YOU . . . GONE . . . CRAZY?" John shouted.

"Animal house!" Vanessa yelled, hiding behind him.

CHAPTER FIVE

Puppies scattered every which way.

The slender, silvery animal disappeared as though it had never been there at all.

Tracker, Jake, and Sheena rocketed through the dog door and high-tailed it for home.

Fritz crouched under the table and hung his head, while the gray puppy got a scolding that she wouldn't soon forget.

"I'm really disappointed in you," John said, along with a lot of other things. "Aren't you happy here, Rosie? Because there's no way a happy puppy could treat her house like this."

"The kitchen doesn't look that bad,"

Vanessa said quickly.

But Rosie knew the kitchen looked terrible. Was the kid sticking up for her? *Or for the silvery animal with the blue collar?*

"We can clean it up fast, Uncle John. I'll help you," Vanessa said.

John sent Rosie and Fritz into the backyard. And for the first time since Rosie had moved in with him, John latched the dog door from inside. She was locked out of her own house!

She and Fritz would have plenty of time to chew over their problems, because it would take the humans much of the afternoon to straighten up the kitchen.

Fritz wheezed and whimpered, feeling sorry for himself.

But Rosie felt like howling at the sun—she was angry!

They were shut out of her house like strays, and they hadn't done anything wrong! But how could they prove it?

The puppies were lying next to each other

under the pine tree when the back door opened quietly. Vanessa bent down to place a handful of something on the top step. Then she tiptoed back inside.

"Chunks of Swiss cheese," Rosie said, sniffing the air. "But we're not taking it."

"Why not? I'm hungry," Fritz whined.

"It's a bribe," Rosie snapped, although she wasn't sure for what. "And stop whining, Fritz!"

"Why should I? I'm the one who'll end up at the animal shelter!" the shepherd puppy moaned.

"We'll run away to Mrs. Foster's house first!" Rosie told him. "Now be quiet—I have to think!"

The day was hot, the air still, and even Rosie grew drowsy . . . until two large, hairy orange shapes suddenly appeared on top of the barbecue pit.

"It's Puffy and Mr. Purr!" Fritz yelped, and scuttled behind the pine tree trunk. "This is the worst day of my life!"

Both cats were grinning toothily.

"What's wrong with the big baby?" Mr. Purr rasped.

"Maybe he could use some company," said Puffy, ready to spring down onto the grass.

But Rosie had had quite enough of animals who had no business on her property. She launched herself straight at the cats, growling ferociously, "Get out of my yard, you fat felines, or I'll . . ."

"Touch-*y*!" Puffy hissed.

"What's happening with you puppies today? Jake and Tracker are all riled up, too," rumbled Mr. Purr.

"Out!" barked Rosie.

"Okay, okay." And the cats hopped down on the far side of the fence.

"Thanks, Rosie," Fritz murmured, slinking back to her side with his tail between his legs.

The two puppies dozed for a while. The grass underneath them was scratchy, and it tickled Rosie's nose. She dreamed that the strange, silvery animal was stretched out on

her pillow in comfort.

When she opened her eyes again, John was walking out of the house with a pet carrier big enough for both puppies in his arms.

Fritz shrieked, "It's the shelter for sure!"

Rosie knew what *that* was like. She'd been there, and she wasn't going back.

Could she reach the fence before John could grab her?

Then John said, "Obedience class for you two. I just hope it'll do you some good."

He loaded the puppies into the carrier: Fritz was moaning and wriggling. Rosie was stiff with rage at the unfairness of it all.

John lifted them into his truck. Vanessa climbed into the front seat beside them. They bounced up the block and around the corner.

At the far end of Main Street, they finally rolled to a stop outside a long wooden building. It was topped with a sign shaped like a Doberman.

"Here we are," John said to Rosie and Fritz. "This is Good Dog Academy. So please

try not to embarrass me."

He opened the carrier and hooked leashes to the puppies' collars. "Once we're inside, Vanessa, I'll hang on to Fritz. And you work with Rosie, okay? There's nothing to be afraid of."

"Sure, Uncle John," Vanessa said softly. Her mind seemed to be somewhere else, even when Rosie flashed her teeth as John lifted her down from the truck.

Tugging on Rosie's and Fritz's leashes, John led them into the building.

A half dozen puppies stood in a row against the far wall of a large room. Each had a human attached to its leash.

The puppies stared at Rosie and Fritz. A couple of them even wagged their tails.

Rosie wagged back, but Fritz whined pitifully and pressed himself against John's legs.

Then a stocky, gray-haired lady hurried over to them. "You must be John Davis," she said. "And these are Rosie and Fritz?"

"That's right. And this is my niece, Vanessa," John said.

"Hello, I'm Alice Mayhew. Why don't you join the others? Just line up behind the man in the blue cap," she told them. "That's right."

"What's going on in here?" Rosie asked the white terrier puppy in front of her.

But Alice Mayhew interrupted. "Please listen, people," she said in a loud voice. "Puppies on your left side, facing front, leash across your body and held in your right hand. Left hand free, slap your left leg, and . . . walk!"

The puppies walked back and forth, across the room and back again, going nowhere, until Rosie was ready to howl with boredom.

"And . . . rest," Alice Mayhew said at last. "People, let your puppies know what excellent jobs they're doing. Pat them and talk to them. Then you may speak to your neighbors if you'd like."

Vanessa stroked Rosie's head cautiously, but she didn't say a word.

As soon as she turned toward John, Rosie asked the white terrier puppy, "So what's the point of all this?"

"No point," the terrier replied. "We walk back and forth, back and forth . . ."

". . . and then we get a dry biscuit—yum," growled a brown puppy next to him. "I'm Spike. So why are you here?"

"Yeah, what kind of trouble did you get into?" a long-haired Lhasa said to Fritz. "I'm Champ."

"We didn't do anything," Fritz whimpered.

"Oh sure—that's everybody's story," said a bulldog puppy. "Like Eddie didn't chew the legs off his living-room couch. . . ."

"Twice," Eddie the white terrier said proudly. He shook himself until his tags jingled merrily.

"And Spike didn't jump on the dining-room table and eat a whole roast," said the Lhasa.

". . . followed by a turkey meatloaf," said Spike, the brown mixed-breed.

"The humans are trying to wear us out, so

that we're too tired to act up at home," explained the bulldog. "But it usually doesn't work."

"Usually the opposite happens," said Champ. "We get all wound up!"

The class didn't make Rosie tired at all—it made her madder.

And this was only the beginning.

"I'll expect all of you tomorrow evening," Alice Mayhew said. "We'll start working on *SIT* and *STAY*."

"I *know* how to sit already," Rosie muttered.

"Doesn't everybody?" said Eddie.

And the puppies had no choice about staying—they were all hooked to leashes.

So what was there to work on?

Alice Mayhew didn't seem very bright. *But lots of humans just don't get it,* Rosie reminded herself.

On the way home, she said to Fritz, "I have to show John how wrong he is about us. Which means finding that silvery critter."

"That animal should be long gone by

now," the shepherd puppy said, sounding hopeful.

"Maybe not," Rosie said. "What if it came into the house when Vanessa did? Maybe . . . maybe that's what I smelled on her hand. Maybe she's the one who bought it that blue collar. And maybe the animal's not leaving until she does."

"You think? It had sharp fangs, and mean black eyes—it looked like a biter!" Fritz whined.

"Do you want it to cause even more trouble for us?" Rosie said. "Or are you going to help me find it?"

Fritz started to tremble.

"I miss Greg and Marcia so much!" the shepherd puppy whimpered. "I just want to go home!"

CHAPTER SIX

That evening Rosie waited until John was snoring loudly. Then she crept over to Fritz's beanbag bed.

She spoke into the shepherd puppy's droopy ear, "Time to search Vanessa's room."

"Oh, Ro-o-osie . . ." Fritz groaned. "Do we have to?"

"We have to!" Rosie said. "I want my life back the way it was."

The steep stairs were hard for the puppies to climb—their hind legs didn't seem to bend in the same way that their front legs did. Rosie slipped downwards almost as often as she pushed herself

upward. But she finally made it to the second floor.

She paused at the top of the stairs, catching her breath, until Fritz flung himself up the last couple of steps.

Then Rosie moved quietly along the upstairs hall, past the spare room where John was sleeping.

She stopped outside a closed door,

telling Fritz, "The kid's in there. I know that you can work doorknobs, so . . ."

"Let's go back down," Fritz pleaded, "before we get caught."

But Rosie was firm. "I'm too short to reach the doorknob, Fritz," she muttered. "You have to."

Finally the shepherd stood up on his back legs. He used his front paws to twist at the knob.

Rosie said, "I'll push. . . ."

Fritz jiggled the knob, and she shoved the door with her shoulder.

At last the door opened a crack.

The puppies peered into the room beyond it. Moonlight was shining through a window onto Vanessa's pillow. Her eyes were closed—she was sound asleep.

Rosie eased into the room and stood perfectly still. At first, all she heard was Vanessa's deep, even breathing. But then her sharp ears picked up a fast *whiish* . . . *whiish* . . . *whiish* sound.

Was it someone—or some*thing*—taking short, fast breaths?

Rosie cocked her head to the side, trying to pinpoint the noise.

When she edged toward a chair piled with Vanessa's clothes, the whishing sound seemed to slow a little.

Rosie picked up a scent: It was the same one she'd smelled on Vanessa's hand!

Excited, she took a step closer to the chair and the clothes. Sure enough, the scent was stronger.

Soon Rosie's nose was only inches away from the chair. Her ears were pricked forward, her tail stiff, her nostrils were twitching. . . .

Suddenly the pile of clothes seemed to explode! A silvery shape burst out of it, and tiny, knife-sharp teeth closed on the tip of the gray puppy's nose.

"Ye-eoow!" Rosie yelped.

She spun in a circle, trying to fling the animal off.

53

"Mmmmfff," Vanessa mumbled, reaching for the lamp next to her bed. "Fergus?"

Rosie had to get out of there!

But the fergus was still clamped to her nose. The pain of it made the puppy's eyes water. She finally knocked the creature loose when she crashed into the edge of the bedroom door.

Rosie could hear Fritz stampeding down the stairs. She took off after him, racing along the hall. She practically tumbled down the steps to the bottom floor.

Above her, John was calling out, "Vanessa, are you all right?"

"It's the shelter for sure!" Fritz yipped, skidding into the kitchen.

He dashed toward the dog door and leaped straight through it.

Rosie thought about jumping through it herself, and hiding out at Mrs. Foster's.

But she didn't really want to leave John.

In the dark kitchen, a low furry shape brushed past her leg.

"Out of my way, you big loser!" a voice squeaked rudely.

The fergus slid through the dog door right in front of Rosie's wounded nose.

Which made up her mind for her in an instant.

"I'll get you!" Rosie growled, and she dove through the dog door.

Everything in the backyard looked different at night—all dim shapes and shadows outlined in silver by the moonlight.

"Where are you?" Rosie rumbled. "Stand and fight, you . . . you fergus!"

"R-Rosie?" Fritz stuttered from behind the barbecue pit.

"That animal's out here somewhere," Rosie told him grimly. "Did you see . . ."

"Out here?"

With one enormous leap, the shepherd puppy sailed all the way over the picket fence. He'd barely landed on the far side of it when he howled in fear. *"Yo-ow-ow-wow!"*

The sound grew fainter as he hurtled up the street.

"The fergus is after him!" Rosie scrambled onto the barbecue pit herself. "I'm coming, Fritz!" She jumped over to the fence rail, and down onto the garbage can.

But it wasn't the fergus who'd spooked Fritz.

Two fat cats were sitting on the hood of a

parked car, big grins on their round faces.

"That was fun," said Puffy.

"Aces," Mr. Purr purred.

"What'll we do next?" Puffy said.

"Terrify those silly parakeets on Mrs. Foster's back porch?" Mr. Purr suggested.

"Sure! Make 'em drop all their feathers!" said Puffy, switching his tail back and forth.

"Listen up! Did you guys see a low, skinny animal run past here?" Rosie growled at them.

"You mean like a weasel?" said Mr. Purr.

"No, a fergus," said Rosie.

Puffy licked his front paw, and Mr. Purr stared up at the moon.

"You wouldn't tell me if you had," said Rosie.

Mr. Purr nodded. "That's right, puppy— we'd just eat it."

"Did you ram your nose into a thornbush?" Puffy asked Rosie.

"Not smart," said Mr. Purr with a smirk.

But Rosie didn't have time to exchange insults. She was already trotting up the street after Fritz.

She figured the shepherd puppy was heading for home, so she turned at the corner.

And pretty soon she could hear him, whining to himself.

"What is that? . . . A bear?" Fritz's voice cracked. "Oh—it's only a clump of grass. . . ." He was trying to hang tough. "Then why is it moving?" The puppy's voice rose even

higher. "The wind . . . Yikes! A *snake!* . . . No, a stick. . . ."

Rosie caught up with Fritz in the alley outside his house.

"I'm not going back to John's tonight, because I'll just get yelled at. I'm staying right here!" the shepherd puppy announced. "But I'm afraid of the dark," he added softly.

"I'll stay with you," Rosie told him.

The puppies scooted under Fritz's fence. They curled up together on his back porch and fell asleep.

CHAPTER SEVEN

Rosie dreamed she chased the fergus all over Buxton, but she never caught him.

When she awoke the next morning, she was worn out and starving.

"Get up, Fritz," she said, poking the shepherd puppy with her sore nose. "Ouch!"

Fritz blinked in the sunlight. "We really slept outside!" he said, surprised but proud of himself.

"I'm hungry," Rosie told him. "It's much too late to find the fergus now, so we might as well get something to eat at John's."

Fritz didn't argue, because he was hungry, too.

They'd barely made it to the corner, however, when they heard Sheena yapping. "Hey-ey-ey!"

The dachshund puppy was barreling down the street toward them, her long hair streaming out behind her.

"Will you help me?" Sheena panted when she reached them.

"Can it wait until after breakfast?" Rosie said.

"No, I have to catch that animal right now! Whatever was at your house has moved over to mine!" said Sheena.

"It's the fergus!" Rosie growled.

Fritz didn't want to have anything more to do with the fergus, but Rosie said, "Sure I'll help. And so will Fritz."

The three puppies crawled back under Fritz's fence and crossed his yard. One by one they stuffed themselves through the hole under Sheena's fence.

They paused on the dachshund's back steps.

"Lucky that Heather left early to run in a marathon," Sheena murmured. Heather was her human. "Can you hear him?"

For a moment all was quiet inside the house. Then there was a thud, followed by a crash.

It sounded like the fergus was busy.

"I'm sick and tired of that little varmint," said Rosie, her lip curling up over her teeth.

She zipped through the dog door, followed by Sheena and finally Fritz.

Heather had a lot of food stored in bags or boxes in her kitchen, and the wicked fergus had

torn into them with its teeth. It had scattered dried fruit and nuts and raisins around the room like confetti.

"It's up there," Sheena told Rosie. "On top of the refrigerator."

The fergus looked bright-eyed and bushy-tailed as it nibbled on a rice cracker—*it* wasn't going hungry.

But Rosie's stomach was rumbling—and so was Rosie!

"Why are you doing all of this, you little creep?" she growled at the fergus.

"Why not? You dogs parade around without a care in the world," the fergus squeaked, "while I'm hidden away in a backpack like a deep, dark secret, living on crumbs—"

"More like chicken wings and roast beef and hard-boiled eggs," Rosie said.

She remembered Vanessa's raids on John's refrigerator.

"—and I have to live on *crumbs*," the fergus repeated crossly, "because Vanessa's mom and dad don't want pets!"

It sent the tin box of rice crackers clattering to the floor.

"Now everyone's going to know when I'm around!" said the fergus. "I'm making sure of that!"

"But you're getting us into a lot of trouble!" Sheena yipped.

"Who cares?" The fergus tossed down a papaya, which just missed the puppies before smashing to yellow mush.

Fritz and Sheena quickly retreated toward the door.

But Rosie held her ground. "I'll shake you like a damp rag!" she snarled.

The little animal cackled. "Cool off— have some wet beans!" It shoved a bowl off the top of the refrigerator with its nose, sending a tidal wave of water and soybeans

splashing across the room.

"At least it can't get out of the kitchen," Sheena said to Rosie. "The door to the dining room is locked."

"So maybe we can corner it!" Rosie said. "Fritz, you're tallest—scare it off the refrigerator."

Fritz whined, "*It* scares *me!*"

"Jump, and growl and bark, like you mean what you say!" Sheena commanded.

"I'll try," Fritz said meekly.

He practiced a couple of growls, low in his throat. Then he hurled himself at the refrigerator, howling hoarsely.

The fergus sprang to the top of the kitchen cabinets and stuck out its pink tongue.

That's when Jake leaped through the dog door.

Tracker arrived a second later.

"We could hear you guys barking a block away!" Jake said.

"Is it burglars?" said Tracker. "What's that smell?"

"It's the fergus again!" said Sheena.

"Hello, losers!" squeaked the fergus.

Rosie's rage pushed her high into the air. She landed on the counter right below the fergus. "Now I'll get you!" she yapped.

If the little animal climbed down, the four puppies on the floor would surround it. And if the fergus stayed where it was, Rosie would soon grab it.

But the fergus fooled them all.

It made a rude squawking noise. Then it dashed along the cabinet tops and slid down the far side, clinging to an apron that was hanging there.

It got stuck for just a moment, when its collar caught on a spoon rack.

But the collar pulled apart, and the fergus hit the floor running.

Flattening out like a lizard, it slipped easily under the dining-room door.

"Rats! It has the whole house to mess up, and we can't do anything!" Sheena yelped.

"All of this is Vanessa's fault!" Rosie

barked, jumping down herself. "She brought the fergus to Buxton, so she'll have to take it away! Come on, Fritz—we're going for the kid!"

Rosie gripped the fergus's blue collar with her teeth and headed for home.

CHAPTER EIGHT

Back in John's kitchen, kibble had already been served in the puppies' food bowls. Rosie and Fritz could hear John talking upstairs.

"Rosie has never run away before," John was saying. "I don't know what's gotten into her!"

He added, "If anything happens to that puppy, I won't ever forgive myself. And if anything happens to Fritz, Greg and Marcia won't forgive me, either. As soon as I shave, we'll start looking around the neighborhood."

Vanessa didn't do anything until the bathroom door had closed. Then she started down the steps, calling softly, "Fergus. Fergus, where are you?"

Tears were running down her face as she hurried into the kitchen.

When she saw Rosie and Fritz standing there, however, she yelled angrily, "What did you puppies do to my ferret?"

"Oh sure, it's our fault!" Rosie rumbled.

The puppy flung the blue collar on the floor in front of the kid.

"This is Fergus's collar!" Vanessa exclaimed, picking it up.

"Grab the leg of her jeans and tug," the gray puppy told Fritz.

Fritz moaned. But he grabbed hold of Vanessa's jeans with his teeth, just like Rosie was doing. They dragged the kid forward a few inches.

"Stop pulling on me!" Vanessa tried to shake them loose.

But Rosie was too angry to shake off, and
Fritz was too strong. The puppies tugged
Vanessa toward the door.

Finally she began to get the idea.

"You want me to go with you, is that it?

Are you taking me to Fergus?" she said at last. "In that case . . ." Vanessa pushed the back door open. "Show me where he is!"

She kept up with Rosie and Fritz as they ran all the way to Sheena's. When the puppies crawled under the fence, Vanessa opened the gate and hurried into the yard, too. But the back door was locked—how could she get into the house?

Vanessa knocked, but no human was there to let her in. And she certainly couldn't fit through the dog door.

So Rosie barked to the dachshund puppy inside, "How do we get her in?"

Sheena yipped back, "Flip up the door mat!"

Rosie stuck her nose under the mat and uncovered a set of door keys.

"I didn't know puppies were smart," Vanessa murmured, reaching for the keys.

She unlocked the back door and called out, "Is anybody home?"

"Wo-o-of!" Tracker yodeled.

But Vanessa hung back. "I could get into major trouble for going inside somebody's . . ." she was saying, when there was a crash and the sound of shattering glass.

"Fergus?" Vanessa jerked the back door open and dashed into Heather's kitchen, with Rosie and Fritz at her heels.

"Wow, what a mess!" Vanessa said, staring at the papaya and crackers and beans.

Then she spotted Sheena, Jake, and Tracker gathered near the closed dining-room door. "Fergus, are you in there?" she shrieked, pushing against it.

She was answered by a high-pitched chittering noise. A few seconds later, the pink tip of a sharp snout appeared at the bottom of the door.

The puppies backed away, but Vanessa fell to her knees and stroked the snout with her finger. "Fergus, it's me! Come on out, boy!"

Fergus the ferret slid neatly under the dining-room door and raced up Vanessa's

arm to perch on her shoulder.

He curved his puffy tail around her neck and chattered into her ear, "I tumbled down some stairs, and I didn't know where I was going, and suddenly I was outdoors in the dark, a giant bird dived at me, I was attacked by two huge hairy animals with mouthfuls of sharp teeth . . ."

"Way to go, Puffy and Mr. Purr," Rosie murmured.

"I slipped into this house to hide from them, and I thought I was safe," Fergus chattered on. "I finally fell asleep. Then these bozos ganged up on me, and . . ."

Vanessa didn't know what he was saying, of course, and she was busy thanking the puppies.

"I couldn't have found him without you guys," she told them. She patted everybody, with an extra pat for Rosie. "I have a feeling I should thank you especially," she said to the gray puppy.

Then Vanessa glanced around the

kitchen and sighed. "Fergus, you've really trashed this place! I better clean it up fast, so we can leave before the owner comes back. Whoever that is."

She was just getting started when John called from outside the house, "Vanessa? Are you in there?"

The ferret disappeared down the neck of Vanessa's T-shirt.

Vanessa muttered, "I'm toast!" But she called back, "Yes, Uncle John! With all of the puppies!"

John opened the back door and stepped inside. "Mrs. Foster told me she saw you headed this way, chasing Rosie and Fritz! Are you okay? Are they?" Then he caught sight of the gray puppy and the black and tan one, peering out at him from behind Vanessa's legs. "They look fine!"

John dropped down on his knees to hug them both. That's when he noticed some of the food that had been flung onto the kitchen floor.

"Did you guys do this?" he said sternly to the puppies. "Where is Heather?"

"Nobody's here," Vanessa said, adding quickly, "the puppies didn't make this mess, Uncle John, or the one at your house, either." She took a deep breath. "The truth is, I have a ferret."

She pulled Fergus out from under her shirt. "See? I got him a few weeks ago from my friend Sara. Mom and Dad don't want any pets, so I've been keeping him hidden. And when I came to stay with you, I brought him with me."

Vanessa glanced around at the five puppies, then looked straight at her uncle. "It's Fergus who's been tearing things up. But I was afraid to tell you because I thought you'd make me get rid of him."

She started to cry. "I d-don't have to, do I?"

"I don't see why you would," John said, putting his arm around Vanessa's shoulder, the one that Fergus wasn't perching on. "He's okay with me. And I'll speak to your

mom and dad about him. We'll be able to work something out, don't worry." He added, "But maybe we should buy him a nice cage, so he won't wreck the place. And some ferret food, and whatever else he needs."

"It's about time!" Fergus chittered from Vanessa's shoulder. "A ferret palace, and food fit for a ferret! I knew I could make them come around."

"Hey, without us, Vanessa never would have even found you, ferret face!" Rosie reminded him from the floor.

"Yeah, well—I guess I owe you," Fergus admitted.

"Big time!" said Rosie.

The five puppies hung out in Sheena's backyard while John and Vanessa cleaned up Heather's kitchen. The humans wrote her a note about the dining room, since they couldn't get in there to see what Fergus had broken.

Then Rosie and Fritz walked home with

John and Vanessa and Fergus. The pups gobbled kibble, John and Vanessa made breakfast, and the ferret lapped up a soft-boiled egg.

Afterward, all of them, including Fergus, piled into John's truck and drove to the pet store just off Main Street.

John asked the owner of Pet Paradise for the fanciest ferret cage in the place: It was a large, two-story cage with a big water bottle, built-in food dishes, and a hammock with a pillow for Fergus to sleep on.

"This is more like it!" Fergus squeaked.

"Just as long as the door locks," Rosie muttered to Fritz.

The ferret tried out the hammock. His beady eyes closed as soon as his pointy little head hit the pillow.

"Look, isn't he cute?" Vanessa whispered to her uncle. "He's all worn out."

She picked up a bag of ferret food and a tube of ferret vitamin paste that smelled like old fish.

Vanessa also chose a red harness for Fergus, with a little bell attached. "So we'll know where he is all the time," she explained to John.

"The kid's smarter than I thought," Rosie told the shepherd puppy.

John let Rosie and Fritz pick out chew toys for themselves. Fritz's was the size of a dinosaur bone!

"Could we get a few more of these?" Vanessa said to her uncle before they headed for the checkout line.

"Chew toys?" John said.

Vanessa nodded. "I'd like to give some to those other puppies—the black puppy and the one with short hair. They were nice," she said. "And the weiner dog."

Rosie looked at Fritz, and their lips stretched into puppy smiles—Sheena definitely wouldn't like to hear herself called a weiner dog. But the kid's heart was in the right place.

"Only a few more days until Vanessa and Fergus are back where they belong," Rosie said to Fritz, around the chew toy in her mouth.

"Only a few more days until Greg and Marcia pick me up," the shepherd puppy agreed with a tail wag.

"Everything's getting back to normal,"

Rosie said cheerfully.

She'd forgotten all about Alice Mayhew's obedience classes.

When Rosie and Fritz woke up from a long nap under the kitchen table that afternoon, they were looking straight at the big pet carrier.

"Yi-i-ipes!" Rosie yipped, scooting backwards on her pillow.

Fritz whimpered and scuttled behind the washing machine.

"Guys, it's time for your obedience class," John said brightly. "I guess you forgot about it in all of the excitement."

Vanessa peered in from the hall. "Do they really have to go, Uncle John? They don't look very happy."

"I think they had a good time yesterday," John said. "Get in the carrier, Rosie. I've paid for three more classes for them both," he explained to Vanessa. "Come on, Fritz— I don't want to argue."

It wasn't until John latched the carrier door and headed out to the truck with them that Rosie realized they weren't alone.

There was a muffled squeak. "Give me some room!" And the ferret popped up in the far corner of the carrier.

"You again!" Rosie yapped.

"*Sssh!*" Fergus hissed at her. "I owe you one, remember? So I'm trying to help you!"

"How are *you* going to help *us?*" Rosie wanted to know.

"I'll figure it out—just get me into the building," said the ferret.

"What building?" Rosie said, not sure what he meant.

"Where you go for these classes!" Fergus said.

Rosie said, "Oh."

But Fritz groaned. "Oh *no!*"

It wasn't that hard for Fergus to sneak into Alice Mayhew's building. The ferret just flattened himself out and scuttled across the parking lot under Rosie's belly.

Once they were safely inside, Fergus muttered to her, "See? Piece of cake. But whatever you do, don't sit down—you'll squash me."

There was that ferret scent, of course.

Rosie heard Eddie the terrier puppy say to the Lhasa, "Hey, Champ, do you smell something funny?"

But Alice Mayhew interrupted. "Listen, people—puppies on the left, leash across to the right hand. Slap your leg with your left hand . . . and WALK!"

Puppies and humans—and one ferret— walked back and forth across the big room for several minutes, back and forth, back and forth . . .

"Bo-o-oring!" Rosie heard Fergus hissing from underneath her.

"No kidding," she agreed grimly. "So why don't you do something?"

"Just waiting for the right time," the ferret muttered.

He didn't wait long.

"Now . . . halt!" Alice Mayhew called out from the other end of the room. "Good dogs! Today we'll be working on *SIT*."

"Uh-oh," Rosie murmured.

"And *STA* . . ." Alice Mayhew didn't get any farther, because that's when Fergus

rocketed out from under Rosie.

As he dashed across the room, every puppy in the place—except Rosie and Fritz—jerked its leash away from its human. Yipping and yapping, the puppies fell all over themselves, trying to catch Fergus. But

the ferret was headed straight for Alice Mayhew.

He scaled her jeans and jacket and grabbed on to her hair. The ferret hoisted himself up to the very top of Alice's gray head before she could do much more than shriek. He stood there, tail flicking, grinning down at all of the crazed puppies who were snarling and snapping and swirling around Alice's feet.

Alice finally found her voice. "Who does this . . . this creature belong to?" she thundered.

"Er. . . uh . . . actually, he's ours," John called out. "I don't know how he got . . ."

"You have ruined hours of successful training!" Alice Mayhew said, striding across the room to where John and Vanessa were standing with Rosie and Fritz. "Get him off me! And please take him—and yourselves— away from here!"

"But . . ." John began, reaching for Fergus.

"Just go!" Alice Mayhew said. "I'll refund your money by mail."

The ferret sprang lightly from Alice's head to Vanessa's shoulder. "Are we even?" Fergus squeaked to Rosie.

"We're even!" the gray puppy said happily.